Reality Untamed

May the Possible Unnerve

a book of haikus by Tonya Mae Howington

Book twelve from the Cryptid Contemplation Series.

Sit. Read one haiku.

Let time pass. Stabilize and

immerse and simmer.

Enjoy.

tonya mae

Reality untamed

May the possible unnerve

Sky we know not

Reality untamed

May the possible unnerve

Sun we know not

Reality untamed

May the possible unnerve

Moon we know not

Reality untamed

May the possible unnerve

Star we know not

Reality untamed

May the possible unnerve

Cloud we know not

Reality untamed

May the possible unnerve

Rain we know not

Reality untamed

May the possible unnerve

Snow we know not

Reality untamed

May the possible unnerve

Wind we know not

∞

Reality untamed

May the possible unnerve

Storm we know not

Reality untamed

May the possible unnerve

Breeze we know not

Reality untamed

May the possible unnerve

Leaf we know not

Reality untamed

May the possible unnerve

Tree we know not

Reality untamed

May the possible unnerve

Grass we know not

Reality untamed

May the possible unnerve

Plant we know not

Reality untamed

May the possible unnerve

Bloom we know not

Reality untamed

May the possible unnerve

Bud we know not

Reality untamed

May the possible unnerve

Root we know not

Reality untamed

May the possible unnerve

Branch we know not

Reality untamed

May the possible unnerve

Twig we know not

Reality untamed

May the possible unnerve

Bush we know not

Reality untamed

May the possible unnerve

Shrub we know not

Reality untamed

May the possible unnerve

Vine we know not

Reality untamed

May the possible unnerve

Moss we know not

Reality untamed

May the possible unnerve

Fern we know not

Reality untamed

May the possible unnerve

Rock we know not

Reality untamed

May the possible unnerve

Stone we know not

Reality untamed

May the possible unnerve

Cliff we know not

Reality untamed

May the possible unnerve

Hill we know not

Reality untamed

May the possible unnerve

Mount we know not

Reality untamed

May the possible unnerve

Peak we know not

Reality untamed

May the possible unnerve

Ridge we know not

Reality untamed

May the possible unnerve

Vale we know not

Reality untamed

May the possible unnerve

Glen we know not

Reality untamed

May the possible unnerve

Stream we know not

Reality untamed

May the possible unnerve

Brook we know not

Reality untamed

May the possible unnerve

Pond we know not

Reality untamed

May the possible unnerve

Lake we know not

Reality untamed

May the possible unnerve

Sea we know not

Reality untamed

May the possible unnerve

Wave we know not

Reality untamed

May the possible unnerve

Tide we know not

Reality untamed

May the possible unnerve

Shore we know not

Reality untamed

May the possible unnerve

Beach we know not

Reality untamed

May the possible unnerve

Sand we know not

Reality untamed

May the possible unnerve

Dune we know not

Reality untamed

May the possible unnerve

Reef we know not

Reality untamed

May the possible unnerve

Shell we know not

Reality untamed

May the possible unnerve

Field we know not

Reality untamed

May the possible unnerve

Grove we know not

Reality untamed

May the possible unnerve

Meadow we know not

Reality untamed

May the possible unnerve

Plain we know not

Reality untamed

May the possible unnerve

Marsh we know not

51

Reality untamed

May the possible unnerve

Swamp we know not

Reality untamed

May the possible unnerve

Bog we know not

Reality untamed

May the possible unnerve

Pine we know not

Reality untamed

May the possible unnerve

Reed we know not

Reality untamed

May the possible unnerve

Spore we know not

Reality untamed

May the possible unnerve

Dust we know not

Reality untamed

May the possible unnerve

Dew we know not

Reality untamed

May the possible unnerve

Moor we know not

Reality untamed

May the possible unnerve

Hail we know not

Reality untamed

May the possible unnerve

Clay we know not

Reality untamed

May the possible unnerve

Seed we know not

Reality untamed

May the possible unnerve

Mud we know not

Reality untamed

May the possible unnerve

Fog we know not

Reality untamed

May the possible unnerve

Fen we know not

Reality untamed

May the possible unnerve

Stem we know not

Reality untamed

May the possible unnerve

Slough we know not

Reality untamed

May the possible unnerve

Space we know not

Reality untamed

May the possible unnerve

Cave we know not

Reality untamed

May the possible unnerve

Bluff we know not

Reality untamed

May the possible unnerve

Bluff we know not

Reality untamed

May the possible unnerve

Bluff we know not

Reality untamed

May the possible unnerve

Bluff we know not

Reality untamed

May the possible unnerve

Bluff we know not

Reality untamed

May the possible unnerve

Bluff we know not

Reality untamed

May the possible unnerve

Bluff we know not

Reality untamed

May the possible unnerve

Bluff we know not

Reality untamed

May the possible unnerve

Bluff we know not

Reality untamed

May the possible unnerve

Bluff we know not

Reality untamed

May the possible unnerve

Bluff we know not

Reality untamed

May the possible unnerve

Bluff we know not

Reality untamed

May the possible unnerve

Bluff we know not

Reality untamed

May the possible unnerve

Bluff we know not

Reality untamed

May the possible unnerve

Bluff we know not

Reality untamed

May the possible unnerve

Bluff we know not

Reality untamed

May the possible unnerve

Bluff we know not

Reality untamed

May the possible unnerve

Bluff we know not

Reality untamed

May the possible unnerve

Bluff we know not

Reality untamed

May the possible unnerve

Bluff we know not

Reality untamed

May the possible unnerve

Bluff we know not

Reality untamed

May the possible unnerve

Bluff we know not

Reality untamed

May the possible unnerve

Bluff we know not

Reality untamed

May the possible unnerve

Bluff we know not

Reality untamed

May the possible unnerve

Bluff we know not

Reality untamed

May the possible unnerve

Bluff we know not

Reality untamed

May the possible unnerve

Bluff we know not

Reality untamed

May the possible unnerve

Bluff we know not

Reality untamed

May the possible unnerve

Bluff we know not

Reality untamed

May the possible unnerve

Bluff we know not

Reality untamed

May the possible unnerve

Bluff we know not

J.F. and J.F. (2023)

www.ingramcontent.com/pod-product-compliance
Lightning Source LLC
Chambersburg PA
CBHW030237180626
46810CB00008B/3170